Alyosha the Pot

*The Quiet Strength of Humility and
Obedience*

A Modern Translation

Adapted for the Contemporary Reader

Leo Tolstoy

Translated by Tim Zengerink

Table of Contents

Preface - Message to the Reader

What If You Could Help Rebuild the Greatest Library in Human History?

Thousands of years ago, the Library of Alexandria stood as the crown jewel of human achievement — a sanctuary where the collected wisdom of every known civilization was gathered, preserved, and shared freely.

And then, it was lost.

Through fire, conquest, and the slow erosion of time, humanity lost not just books — but ideas, dreams, discoveries, and stories that could have changed the world forever.

Today, the Library of Alexandria lives again — and you are invited to be a part of its restoration.

Our mission is simple yet profound:

To rebuild the greatest library the world has ever known, and to translate all timeless works into every language and dialect, so that no seeker of knowledge is ever left behind again.

By joining our movement to rebuild the modern Library of Alexandria, you become part of an unprecedented mission:

- **Unlimited Access to the Greatest Audiobooks & eBooks Ever Written:**

  Instantly explore thousands of legendary works—Plato, Shakespeare, Jane Austen, Leo Tolstoy, and countless more. All instantly available to read or listen, placing a complete literary universe at your fingertips.

- **Beautiful Paperback & Deluxe Editions at Printing Cost**

  Own any title as an elegant paperback, deluxe hardcover, or stunning collectible boxset—offered to you at true printing cost, delivered straight to your door. Build your personal Library of Alexandria, crafted for beauty, built for durability, and worthy of proud display.

- **Fresh Translations for Modern Readers—in Every Language & Dialect**

  Enjoy timeless masterpieces reimagined in clear, contemporary language—no more outdated phrases or obscure references. Alongside the original versions, we're tirelessly translating these classics into every language and dialect imaginable, ensuring accessibility and understanding across cultures and generations.

- **Join a Global Renaissance of Literature & Knowledge**

  You directly support expanding our library, publishing deluxe editions at true cost, translating works into all global languages, and bringing humanity's greatest stories to people everywhere. By joining today, you're not just preserving a legacy of masterpieces; you set in motion a powerful wave of literary accessibility.

Become a Torchbearer of Knowledge.

Join us for free now at **LibraryofAlexandria.com**

Together, we will ensure that the light of human wisdom never fades again.

With gratitude and a shared love of knowledge,

The Modern Library of Alexandria Team

Visit:

www.libraryofalexandria.com

Or scan the code below:

Introduction

The Holiness of the Ordinary:
Tolstoy's Tribute to Obedience and Silent Virtue

Leo Tolstoy's Alyosha the Pot is a story of striking brevity, simplicity, and spiritual depth. Written in the last year of his life in 1910, this short tale serves as a final testament to the author's mature religious and philosophical beliefs. It is the story of Alyosha, a poor, quiet, and humble servant boy whose life is outwardly insignificant—he is obedient, unnoticed, and meek. Yet, in the spiritual economy that Tolstoy came to espouse in his final years, Alyosha is a saint. He is a figure of profound moral clarity and inner peace, a man who achieves grace not through greatness but through simplicity and sacrifice.

Tolstoy, who had by this point renounced wealth, fame, the Russian Orthodox Church, and his former aristocratic life, offers Alyosha as the embodiment of his vision of Christian humility. The story critiques not only the materialistic and hierarchical structures of Russian society but also the ways in which institutional religion often overlooks the spiritual purity of the simple and meek. In Alyosha, we see a kind of living parable—a soul that fulfills Christ's Beatitudes not through grand gestures but through patient suffering, quiet service, and absolute obedience.

Though the story is only a few pages long, its impact is enduring. It has been praised for its understated power, its moral subtlety, and its stark contrast to the heroism and drama found in more conventional narratives. There are no miracles in Alyosha the Pot, no dramatic conversions or revelations. There is only a boy who lives quietly, loves purely, and dies without complaint. And in that, Tolstoy finds the essence of holiness.

A Life of Service, A Death Without Complaint:
The Gospel in Action

The story begins with a simple act of familial duty. Alyosha, nicknamed "the Pot" by his classmates for his awkward appearance and clumsy demeanor, is sent by his father to replace his deceased older brother in the service of a local merchant. Alyosha performs his tasks without question. He wakes early, works hard, eats little, and never complains. His master, recognizing his obedience, trusts him. His fellow servants tease him. The cook eventually falls in love with him, and for a brief moment, the possibility of personal happiness flickers into view.

But it is quickly extinguished. When the merchant discovers that Alyosha and the cook are growing close, he forbids the match, and Alyosha quietly obeys. He offers no resistance, no argument, no sadness. When asked why he does not speak up for himself, Alyosha simply says that it's not his place. This response baffles those around him, but it reveals the central theme of the story: the spiritual strength found in surrender.

To modern readers, Alyosha's meekness may appear as passivity or even servility. But Tolstoy does not present him as a fool or a coward. Rather, he is a man who has renounced ego, pride, and ambition. He does not seek to impose his will on the world. He accepts his lot with gratitude and serenity, embodying a kind of radical obedience that transcends fear or hope. His love, though denied, leaves no bitterness. His death, caused by a fall from a roof while serving his master, is met with the same silence with which he lived.

In death, as in life, Alyosha asks for nothing and leaves nothing behind—except a question in the minds of those who knew him. What kind of life was this? Was it wasted or holy? For Tolstoy, the answer is clear. Alyosha's life, though invisible to the world, was rich in the currency of the spirit. His obedience was not weakness but strength. His silence was not ignorance but wisdom. His death was not a loss but a quiet entry into eternal peace.

This modern translation of Alyosha the Pot aims to preserve the quiet intensity and moral clarity of the original while making the language accessible and emotionally resonant for contemporary readers. Every line has been carefully rendered to reflect the tone of gentle compassion and quiet awe that runs through Tolstoy's final vision of what it means to live rightly.

In conclusion, Alyosha the Pot is not simply a story—it is a meditation. It invites us to reimagine what it means to be strong, what it means to love, and what it means to live a good life. In an age obsessed with achievement, recognition, and personal fulfillment, Tolstoy's Alyosha offers an alternative model of human dignity: one grounded in humility, obedience, and quiet faithfulness. It is a call to notice the holy in the ordinary, the light in the unnoticed, and the grace that often passes without spectacle or acclaim.

Alyosha The Pot

Alyosha was the youngest child in his family. People gave him the nickname "Pot" because, when he was little, his mother sent him to deliver a pot of milk to the deacon's wife. On the way, he tripped and dropped it, spilling everything. His mother scolded him, and the other children teased him about it so much that the name stuck. From that day on, everyone called him "Pot."

He was small and thin, with ears that stuck out and a large nose. The other kids made fun of him, joking, "Alyosha's nose looks like a dog sitting on a hill!" He went to the village school, but he struggled with his lessons and didn't have much time to study. His older brother had moved to the city to work for a merchant, so Alyosha had to start helping his father at a young age.

By the time he was six, he was already going to the fields with the girls to watch over the cows and sheep. A little later, he started taking care of the horses, both during the day and at night. By the age of twelve, he was plowing the fields and driving carts. He didn't have much strength, but he was skilled.

No matter how hard life was, Alyosha was always cheerful. When the other children made fun of him, he either laughed along or stayed quiet. When his father scolded him, he stood still and listened, never arguing. As soon as the scolding ended, he smiled and went back to work.

When he was nineteen, his older brother was drafted into the army. So, their father sent Alyosha to take his place working for the merchant. He was given his brother's old boots, his father's worn-out coat and cap, and was taken to the city. Alyosha was excited about his new clothes, but the merchant wasn't impressed.

"I expected you to bring me a proper worker to take Simeon's place," the merchant said, looking Alyosha up and down. "But you bring me this? What can he possibly do?"

"He can do it all," his father replied. "He knows how to handle horses, he can drive, and he works hard. He might look small, but he's strong. And he's eager to work."

The merchant raised an eyebrow. "Well, he certainly looks eager. Alright, we'll see what he's capable of."

And so, Alyosha started working for the merchant.

The family wasn't very big. There was the merchant himself, his wife, and her elderly mother. They had a married son who worked in the family business but wasn't very smart. Another son had gone to university but had been expelled and now lived at home. They also had a daughter who was still in school.

At first, nobody in the house liked Alyosha. He was rough, poorly dressed, and didn't know how to act around them. But soon, they got used to him because he worked even harder than his brother had. He was always ready to help and never said no.

They sent him on endless errands, and he did them all quickly, moving from one task to the next without rest. Soon, just like at home, all the hardest jobs fell on his shoulders. The more work he did, the more they gave him. The merchant's wife, the old grandmother, the sons, the daughter, the clerk, and even the cook—everyone bossed him around.

"Alyosha, go here! Alyosha, do that! Did you forget, Alyosha? Make sure you remember!"

From morning until night, people were always calling his name. He rushed from one task to another, never forgetting anything and always managing to get everything done. No matter how much work he had, he remained cheerful.

His brother's old boots soon wore out, and the merchant scolded him for walking around with his toes sticking out. He told someone to buy a new pair for him at the market. Alyosha was happy with his new boots, but his feet ached from all the running. He also worried that his father would be angry when he found out that part of his wages had been used to pay for them.

During the winter, Alyosha woke up before sunrise. He chopped firewood, swept the yard, fed the cows and horses, started the stoves, shined boots, and set up the samovar for tea. If the clerk needed something, he ran to get it. If the cook needed help, he kneaded dough and scrubbed pots. After that, he rushed into town to run errands, picked up the merchant's daughter from school, or bought olive oil for the grandmother.

"Why did it take you so long?" someone would always scold him.

Why should anyone else go? Alyosha could handle it. "Alyosha! Alyosha!"

He grabbed quick bites of food while he worked, rarely eating meals on time. The cook often scolded him for being late, but she also felt sorry for him and would keep his food warm.

Holidays meant even more work, but Alyosha still liked them because people gave him small tips. It wasn't much, but by the end of the day, he would have about sixty kopeks—all his own money. Alyosha never saw his real wages. His father collected them from the merchant and only scolded him for wearing out his boots too fast.

After saving up two rubles, the cook suggested he buy a red knitted jacket. When he put it on, he was so happy that he couldn't stop smiling.

Alyosha didn't talk much. When he did, his words were short and to the point. He always answered "yes" without hesitation and got straight to work.

He didn't know any prayers. He had forgotten what his mother had taught him, but he still prayed in his own way—every morning and night, he crossed himself with his hands.

He lived this way for about a year and a half. Then, something happened that changed him completely.

One day, Alyosha realized something new—people weren't only valued for the work they did. Sometimes, someone cared about a person just because they wanted to, not because they needed anything from them.

He learned this from Ustinia, the cook. She was young, had no family, and worked as hard as he did. For the first time, Alyosha felt like he was important—not because of his chores, but just for being himself.

When his mother had been kind to him, he hadn't thought much about it. That was just what mothers did. But Ustinia was different. She wasn't family, yet she still cared.

She would save warm porridge for him and sit nearby as he ate, resting her chin on her bare arm with her sleeve rolled up. If he looked at her, she would giggle. And every time, he found himself smiling back.

This was something completely new to Alyosha, and it scared him a little. He worried it might distract him from his work. But at the same time, it made him happy. When he saw the pants Ustinia had patched for him, he would shake his head and smile. He often thought about her while working or running errands. Sometimes, he would quietly say to himself, "Ustinia is such a good girl."

Ustinia helped Alyosha whenever she could, and he did the same for her. She shared stories about her life—how she had lost her parents, how her aunt took her in and helped her find a job in town, and how the merchant's son had tried to bother her, but she had stood up for herself. Ustinia liked to talk, and Alyosha liked listening to her.

He had heard that peasants who moved to the city often married servant girls. One day, she asked him if his parents planned to find him a wife soon.

"I don't know," he said. "I don't really want to marry any of the village girls."

"Do you already like someone, then?" she asked.

"I'd marry you if you'd have me," he said simply.

She laughed and playfully swatted his back with a towel. "Well, look at that! Alyosha the Pot has finally learned how to talk!"

At Shrovetide, Alyosha's father came to town to collect his wages. The merchant's wife had heard about Alyosha wanting to marry Ustinia, and she didn't approve. "What good will she be if she gets pregnant?" she thought. She told her husband about it.

When the merchant handed Alyosha's wages to his father, he said, "So, how is the boy doing? I told you he'd be hardworking."

"He's doing fine, but he's got some silly idea in his head. He wants to marry our cook. I don't allow married servants in my house."

His father was shocked. "That fool? Thinking about marriage? Don't worry—I'll put a stop to that."

He went to the kitchen and sat at the table, waiting for Alyosha to return. When Alyosha came back from an errand, out of breath, his father began talking right away.

"I thought you had some sense. What nonsense is this?"

"What do you mean?" Alyosha asked.

"They say you want to get married. You'll marry when the time is right. And it won't be some town girl."

His father kept talking while Alyosha just stood there, listening and sighing. When his father finally finished, Alyosha smiled and said, "Alright. I'll forget about it."

"Now that's what I call good sense," his father said, satisfied.

Later, when Alyosha was alone with Ustinia, he told her what had happened. She had already been listening at the door.

"It won't work," he said. "Did you hear him? He's against it. It won't happen."

Ustinia buried her face in her apron and started crying.

Alyosha shook his head. "What can we do? We have to listen to them."

That evening, as he closed the shutters, his mistress asked, "So, have you given up on that foolishness like your father told you?"

"Of course," Alyosha said with a smile. Then, suddenly, he started crying.

After that, Alyosha continued working as usual and never mentioned marriage to Ustinia again.

One day during Lent, the clerk asked Alyosha to clear the snow off the roof. He climbed up and started shoveling. As he was scraping away some frozen chunks from the gutter, his foot suddenly slipped. He lost his balance and fell—not onto the soft snow, but onto a hard piece of iron near the door.

Ustinia and the merchant's daughter ran to him.

"Alyosha! Are you hurt?" Ustinia asked.

He tried to lift himself but couldn't. He gave a small smile. "No, it's nothing."

They carried him inside to the servants' quarters. The doctor arrived and examined him.

"Where does it hurt?" he asked.

"Everywhere," Alyosha said. "But it doesn't matter. I'm just worried the master will be upset. My father should be told."

Alyosha stayed in bed for two days. On the third day, they called for the priest.

"Are you really going to die?" Ustinia asked him.

"Of course. No one lives forever. When it's your time, you have to go," Alyosha said, talking fast like he always did. Then he added, "Thank you, Ustinia. You were always good to me. It's probably for the best that they didn't let us marry. What would we have done then? This way is easier."

When the priest arrived, Alyosha prayed—first with his hands, then with his heart.

"As it is good here to listen and not hurt others, it must be good there too," he thought.

He didn't say much after that. He only mentioned being thirsty, and his face was filled with quiet wonder, as if he had just realized something.

He lay there, staring in amazement. Then, he stretched out his body and took his last breath.

Thank You for Reading

Dear Reader,

We hope this timeless classic has sparked your imagination and enriched your literary journey. Now that you've turned the final page, we want to share a vision for the future of reading—one where every classic you've ever wanted to explore is at your fingertips, in a format that best suits your life.

We'd like to invite you to gain immediate, unlimited digital & audiobook access to hundreds of the most treasured literary classics ever written—along with the option to secure deluxe paperback, hardcover & box set editions at printing cost. Together, we can spark a new global literary renaissance alongside our small, independent publishing house called "The Library of Alexandria."

Thousands of years ago, the Library of Alexandria stood as a beacon of knowledge—until it was lost to history. We aim to reignite that spirit of preservation and discovery right now, in the modern age—only this time, it's accessible to all, in every language and every format.

Picture a world where every timeless classic, novel, poem, or philosophical treatise is not only available to read but also updated for today's readers—modernized, translated into any language or dialect, and ready to enjoy in any format you choose, whether that is in an eBook, audiobook, paperback, or deluxe hardcover & box set version a printing cost.

By joining our movement to rebuild the modern Library of Alexandria, you become part of an unprecedented mission to offer:

- **Unlimited Audiobook & eBook Access to the Greatest Classics of All Time**

  Instantly explore thousands of legendary works, from Plato and Shakespeare to Jane Austen and Leo Tolstoy. All are instantly ready to read or listen to, giving you a complete literary universe at your fingertips.

- **Paperback & Deluxe Editions at Printing Costs:**

  Purchase any title in a paperback, deluxe hardbound, or deluxe boxset edition at printing costs, shipped right to your doorstep. Curate your personal library of Alexandria with editions worthy of display— crafted to last, designed to captivate, and delivered straight to your door.

- **Modern translations for Contemporary Readers in all languages and dialects**

  Discover a vast selection of classics reimagined in clear, current language—no more struggling with outdated phrases or obscure references. Next to the original versions, we aim to offer translations in as many languages and dialects as possible.

  As we continue our translation efforts and add new languages, readers everywhere can connect with these works as if they were written today. By bridging linguistic divides, you're contributing to ensuring that these timeless stories become more meaningful, accessible, and inspiring for people across the globe.

- **Your Personal Library of Alexandria:**

  Over the months and years, you'll curate a unique physical archive of classics—each volume a testament to your taste, curiosity, and love of knowledge. It's not just about owning books—it's about curating a cultural legacy you'll cherish and pass down for generations to come.

- **Join a Global Literary Renaissance:**

  Your support fuels an ongoing mission: allowing us to reinvest in offering deluxe print editions (including special boxsets) at their true cost, broaden the range of available formats and translations, and extend the reach of these works to new audiences worldwide. By joining today, you're not just preserving a legacy of masterpieces; you set in motion a powerful wave of literary accessibility.

We are more than a publisher—we're a movement, and we can't do it alone. Your support lets us scale our mission, preserving and reimagining history's greatest works for tomorrow's readers.

Become a Torchbearer of knowledge.

Thank you for picking up this book and allowing us into your literary journey. As you turn the pages, know that you're part of something larger: a global effort to keep these stories alive, share their wisdom across borders and generations, and spark a true cultural revival for the modern era.

If this resonates with you—please consider taking the next step by visiting:

www.libraryofalexandria.com

With gratitude and a shared love of knowledge,

The Modern Library of Alexandria Team

Visit:

www.libraryofalexandria.com

Or scan the code below: